I hope you enjoy these 'tales' & characters as much as I did when I was a little girl.

Love,

Aunt Jan

TALES FROM
BEATRIX POTTER

TALES FROM
BEATRIX POTTER

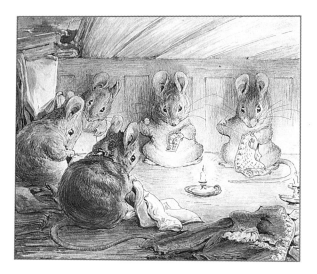

THE ORIGINAL AND AUTHORIZED EDITIONS

BY BEATRIX POTTER ™

New colour reproductions

F. WARNE & Co.

FREDERICK WARNE
Published by the Penguin Group
27 Wrights Lane, London w8 5TZ, England
Viking Penguin Inc., 40 West 23rd Street, New York, New York 10010, USA
Penguin Books Australia Ltd, Ringwood, Victoria, Australia
Penguin Books Canada Ltd, 2801 John Street, Markham, Ontario, Canada L3R 1B4
Penguin Books (NZ) Ltd, 182–190 Wairau Road, Auckland 10, New Zealand

Penguin Books Ltd, Registered Offices: Harmondsworth, Middlesex, England

First published in this format 1984
Reprinted 1985 and 1986
This edition with new reproductions first published 1987
Reprinted 1988

ISBN 0 7232 3971 1

Colour reproduction by
East Anglian Engraving Company Limited, Norwich
Printed and bound in Great Britain by
William Clowes Limited, Beccles and London

Contents

THE TAILOR OF GLOUCESTER

IN the time of swords and periwigs
and full-skirted coats with flowered
lappets—when gentlemen wore ruffles,
and gold-laced waistcoats of paduasoy
and taffeta—there lived a tailor in
Gloucester.

He sat in the window of a little
shop in Westgate Street, cross-legged
on a table, from morning till dark.

All day long while the light lasted
he sewed and snippeted, piecing out
his satin and pompadour, and lute-

string; stuffs had strange names, and were very expensive in the days of the Tailor of Gloucester.

But although he sewed fine silk for his neighbours, he himself was very, very poor—a little old man in spectacles, with a pinched face, old crooked fingers, and a suit of thread-bare clothes.

He cut his coats without waste, according to his embroidered cloth; they were very small ends and snippets that lay about upon the table—'Too narrow breadths for nought—except waistcoats for mice,' said the tailor.

One bitter cold day near Christmas-time the tailor began to make a coat—a coat of cherry-coloured corded silk embroidered with pansies and roses, and a cream coloured satin waistcoat—trimmed with gauze and green worsted chenille—for the Mayor of Gloucester.

The tailor worked and worked, and he talked to himself. He measured the silk, and turned it round and round, and trimmed it into shape with his

shears; the table was all littered with cherry-coloured snippets.

'No breadth at all, and cut on the cross; it is no breadth at all; tippets for mice and ribbons for mobs! for mice!' said the Tailor of Gloucester.

When the snow-flakes came down against the small leaded window-panes and shut out the light, the tailor had done his day's work; all the silk and satin lay cut out upon the table.

There were twelve pieces for the coat and four pieces for the waistcoat; and

there were pocket flaps and cuffs, and
buttons all in order. For the lining of
the coat there was fine yellow taffeta;
and for the button-holes of the waist-
coat, there was cherry-coloured twist.
And everything was ready to sew
together in the morning, all measured
and sufficient—except that there was
wanting just one single skein of cherry-
coloured twisted silk.

The tailor came out of his shop at
dark, for he did not sleep there at

nights; he fastened the window and locked the door, and took away the key. No one lived there at night but little brown mice, and they run in and out without any keys!

For behind the wooden wainscots of all the old houses in Gloucester, there are little mouse staircases and secret trap-doors; and the mice run from house to house through those long narrow passages; they can run all over the town without going into the streets.

But the tailor came out of his shop,
and shuffled home through the snow.
He lived quite near by in College
Court, next the doorway to College
Green; and although it was not a big
house, the tailor was so poor he only
rented the kitchen.

He lived alone with his cat; it was
called Simpkin.

Now all day long while the tailor
was out at work, Simpkin kept house
by himself; and he also was fond of

the mice, though he gave them no
satin for coats!

'Miaw?' said the cat when the tailor
opened the door. 'Miaw?'

The tailor replied—'Simpkin, we
shall make our fortune, but I am worn
to a ravelling. Take this groat (which
is our last fourpence) and Simpkin,
take a china pipkin; buy a penn'orth
of bread, a penn'orth of milk and a
penn'orth of sausages. And oh, Simpkin, with the last penny of our four-

pence buy me one penn'orth of cherry-coloured silk. But do not lose the last penny of the fourpence, Simpkin, or I am undone and worn to a threadpaper, for I have NO MORE TWIST.'

Then Simpkin again said, 'Miaw?' and took the groat and the pipkin, and went out into the dark.

The tailor was very tired and beginning to be ill. He sat down by the hearth and talked to himself about that wonderful coat.

'I shall make my fortune—to be cut bias—the Mayor of Gloucester is to be married on Christmas Day in the morning, and he hath ordered a coat and an embroidered waistcoat—to be lined with yellow taffeta—and the taffeta sufficeth; there is no more left over in snippets than will serve to make tippets for mice—'

Then the tailor started; for suddenly, interrupting him, from the dresser at the other side of the kitchen came a

number of little noises—

Tip tap, tip tap, tip tap tip!

'Now what can that be?' said the Tailor of Gloucester, jumping up from his chair. The dresser was covered with crockery and pipkins, willow pattern plates, and tea-cups and mugs.

The tailor crossed the kitchen, and stood quite still beside the dresser, listening, and peering through his spectacles. Again from under a tea-cup, came those funny little noises—

Tip tap, tip tap, tip tap tip!

'This is very peculiar,' said the Tailor of Gloucester; and he lifted up the tea-cup which was upside down.

Out stepped a little live lady mouse, and made a curtsey to the tailor! Then she hopped away down off the dresser, and under the wainscot.

The tailor sat down again by the fire, warming his poor cold hands, and mumbling to himself—

'The waistcoat is cut out from peach-coloured satin—tambour stitch and rose-buds in beautiful floss silk. Was I

wise to entrust my last fourpence to Simpkin? One-and-twenty button-holes of cherry-coloured twist!'

But all at once, from the dresser, there came other little noises:

Tip tap, tip tap, tip tap tip!

'This is passing extraordinary!' said the Tailor of Gloucester, and turned over another tea-cup, which was upside down.

Out stepped a little gentleman mouse, and made a bow to the tailor!

And then from all over the dresser came a chorus of little tappings, all sounding together, and answering one another, like watch-beetles in an old worm-eaten window-shutter—

Tip tap, tip tap, tip tap tip!

And out from under tea-cups and from under bowls and basins, stepped other and more little mice who hopped away down off the dresser and under the wainscot.

The tailor sat down, close over the

fire, lamenting—'One-and-twenty button-holes of cherry-coloured silk! To
be finished by noon of Saturday: and
this is Tuesday evening. Was it right
to let loose those mice, undoubtedly
the property of Simpkin? Alack, I am
undone, for I have no more twist!'

The little mice came out again, and
listened to the tailor; they took notice of
the pattern of that wonderful coat. They
whispered to one another about the taffeta lining, and about little mouse tippets.

And then all at once they all ran away together down the passage behind the wainscot, squeaking and calling to one another, as they ran from house to house; and not one mouse was left in the tailor's kitchen when Simpkin came back with the pipkin of milk!

Simpkin opened the door and bounced in, with an angry 'G-r-r-miaw!' like a cat that is vexed: for he hated the snow, and there was snow in his ears, and snow in his collar at

the back of his neck. He put down the
loaf and the sausages upon the dresser,
and sniffed.

'Simpkin,' said the tailor, 'where is
my twist?'

But Simpkin set down the pipkin of
milk upon the dresser, and looked
suspiciously at the tea-cups. He wanted
his supper of little fat mouse!

'Simpkin,' said the tailor, 'where is
my TWIST?'

But Simpkin hid a little parcel privately in the tea-pot, and spit and growled at the tailor; and if Simpkin had been able to talk, he would have asked: 'Where is my MOUSE?'

'Alack, I am undone!' said the Tailor of Gloucester, and went sadly to bed.

All that night long Simpkin hunted and searched through the kitchen, peeping into cupboards and under the wainscot, and into the tea-pot where he had hidden that twist; but still he found never a mouse!

Whenever the tailor muttered and talked in his sleep, Simpkin said 'Miaw-ger-r-w-s-s-ch!' and made strange horrid noises, as cats do at night.

For the poor old tailor was very ill with a fever, tossing and turning in his four-post bed; and still in his dreams he mumbled—'No more twist! no more twist!'

All that day he was ill, and the next day, and the next; and what should become of the cherry-coloured coat? In

the tailor's shop in Westgate Street the
embroidered silk and satin lay cut out
upon the table—one-and-twenty button-
holes—and who should come to sew
them, when the window was barred,
and the door was fast locked?

But that does not hinder the little
brown mice; they run in and out
without any keys through all the old
houses in Gloucester!

Out of doors the market folks went
trudging through the snow to buy their

geese and turkeys, and to bake their
Christmas pies; but there would be no
Christmas dinner for Simpkin and the
poor old Tailor of Gloucester.

The tailor lay ill for three days and
nights; and then it was Christmas Eve,
and very late at night. The moon
climbed up over the roofs and chim-
neys, and looked down over the gate-
way into College Court. There were
no lights in the windows, nor any
sound in the houses; all the city of

Gloucester was fast asleep under the snow.

And still Simpkin wanted his mice, and he mewed as he stood beside the four-post bed.

But it is in the old story that all the beasts can talk, in the night between Christmas Eve and Christmas Day in the morning (though there are very few folk that can hear them, or know what it is that they say).

When the Cathedral clock struck twelve there was an answer—like an echo of the chimes—and Simpkin heard it, and came out of the tailor's door, and wandered about in the snow.

From all the roofs and gables and old wooden houses in Gloucester came a thousand merry voices singing the old Christmas rhymes—all the old songs that ever I heard of, and some that I don't know, like Whittington's bells.

First and loudest the cocks cried out: 'Dame, get up, and bake your pies!'

'Oh, dilly, dilly, dilly!' sighed Simpkin.

And now in a garret there were
lights and sounds of dancing, and cats
came from over the way.

'Hey, diddle, diddle, the cat and the
fiddle! All the cats in Gloucester—
except me,' said Simpkin.

Under the wooden eaves the starlings
and sparrows sang of Christmas pies;
the jack-daws woke up in the Cathedral
tower; and although it was the middle
of the night the throstles and robins

sang; the air was quite full of little
twittering tunes.

But it was all rather provoking to
poor hungry Simpkin!

Particularly he was vexed with some
little shrill voices from behind a
wooden lattice. I think that they were
bats, because they always have very
small voices—especially in a black frost,
when they talk in their sleep, like the
Tailor of Gloucester.

They said something mysterious that

sounded like—

'Buz, quoth the blue fly; hum, quoth the bee;
Buz and hum they cry, and so do we!'

and Simpkin went away shaking his ears as if he had a bee in his bonnet.

From the tailor's shop in Westgate came a glow of light; and when Simpkin crept up to peep in at the window it was full of candles. There was a snippeting of scissors, and snappeting of thread; and little mouse voices sang loudly and gaily—

'Four-and-twenty tailors
Went to catch a snail,
The best man amongst them
Durst not touch her tail;
She put out her horns
Like a little kyloe cow,
Run, tailors, run! or she'll have you all e'en now!'

Then without a pause the little mouse voices went on again—

'Sieve my lady's oatmeal,
Grind my lady's flour,
Put it in a chestnut,
Let it stand an hour—'

'Mew! Mew!' interrupted Simpkin, and he scratched at the door. But the key was under the tailor's pillow, he

could not get in.

The little mice only laughed, and
tried another tune—

'Three little mice sat down to spin,
Pussy passed by and she peeped in.
What are you at, my fine little men?
Making coats for gentlemen.
Shall I come in and cut off your threads?
Oh, no, Miss Pussy, you'd bite off our heads!'

'Mew! Mew!' cried Simpkin. 'Hey
diddle dinketty?' answered the little
mice—

'Hey diddle dinketty, poppetty pet!
The merchants of London they wear scarlet;
Silk in the collar, and gold in the hem,
So merrily march the merchantmen!'

They clicked their thimbles to mark
the time, but none of the songs pleased
Simpkin; he sniffed and mewed at the
door of the shop.

'And then I bought
A pipkin and a popkin,
A slipkin and a slopkin,
All for one farthing—

and upon the kitchen dresser!' added
the rude little mice.

'Mew! scratch! scratch!' scuffled
Simpkin on the window-sill; while the
little mice inside sprang to their feet,
and all began to shout at once in little

twittering voices: 'No more twist! No more twist!' And they barred up the window shutters and shut out Simpkin.

But still through the nicks in the shutters he could hear the click of thimbles, and little mouse voices singing—

'No more twist! No more twist!'

Simpkin came away from the shop and went home, considering in his mind. He found the poor old tailor without fever, sleeping peacefully.

Then Simpkin went on tip-toe and took a little parcel of silk out of the tea-pot, and looked at it in the moon-light; and he felt quite ashamed of his badness compared with those good little mice!

When the tailor awoke in the morning, the first thing which he saw upon the patchwork quilt, was a skein of cherry-coloured twisted silk, and beside his bed stood the repentant Simpkin!

'Alack, I am worn to a ravelling,' said the Tailor of Gloucester, 'but I have my twist!'

The sun was shining on the snow when the tailor got up and dressed, and came out into the street with Simpkin running before him.

The starlings whistled on the chimney stacks, and the throstles and robins sang—but they sang their own little noises, not the words they had sung in the night.

'Alack,' said the tailor, 'I have my twist; but no more strength—nor time—than will serve to make me one

single button-hole; for this is Christmas Day in the Morning! The Mayor of Gloucester shall be married by noon— and where is his cherry-coloured coat?'

He unlocked the door of the little shop in Westgate Street, and Simpkin ran in, like a cat that expects something.

But there was no one there! Not even one little brown mouse!

The boards were swept clean; the little ends of thread and the little silk snippets were all tidied away, and gone from off the floor.

But upon the table—oh joy! the tailor gave a shout—there, where he had left plain cuttings of silk—there lay the most beautifullest coat and embroidered satin waistcoat that ever were worn by a Mayor of Gloucester.

There were roses and pansies upon the facings of the coat; and the waist-coat was worked with poppies and corn-flowers.

Everything was finished except just one single cherry-coloured button-hole, and where that button-hole was wanting there was pinned a scrap of paper with these words—in little teeny weeny writing—

NO MORE TWIST

And from then began the luck of the Tailor of Gloucester; he grew quite stout, and he grew quite rich.

He made the most wonderful waist-coats for all the rich merchants of

Gloucester, and for all the fine gentlemen of the country round.

Never were seen such ruffles, or such
embroidered cuffs and lappets! But his
button-holes were the greatest triumph
of it all.

The stitches of those button-holes
were so neat—*so* neat—I wonder how
they could be stitched by an old man
in spectacles, with crooked old fingers,
and a tailor's thimble.

The stitches of those button-holes were so small—*so* small—they looked as if they had been made by little mice!

THE TALE OF
MRS. TIGGY~WINKLE

ONCE upon a time there was a little girl called Lucie, who lived at a farm called Little-town. She was a good little girl—only she was always losing her pocket-handkerchiefs!

One day little Lucie came into the farm-yard crying—oh, she did cry so! 'I've lost my pocket-handkin! Three handkins and a pinny! Have *you* seen them, Tabby Kitten?'

THE Kitten went on washing her white paws; so Lucie asked a speckled hen—

'Sally Henny-penny, have *you* found three pocket-handkins?'

But the speckled hen ran into a barn, clucking—

'I go barefoot, barefoot, barefoot!'

AND then Lucie asked Cock Robin sitting on a twig.

Cock Robin looked sideways at Lucie with his bright black eye, and he flew over a stile and away.

Lucie climbed upon the stile and looked up at the hill behind Little-town—a hill that goes up—up—into the clouds as though it had no top!

And a great way up the hill-side she thought she saw some white things spread upon the grass.

LUCIE scrambled up the hill as fast as her stout legs would carry her; she ran along a steep path-way—up and up—until Little-town was right away down below—she could have dropped a pebble down the chimney!

P RESENTLY she came to a spring, bubbling out from the hill-side.

Some one had stood a tin can upon a stone to catch the water—but the water was already running over, for the can was no bigger than an egg-cup! And where the sand upon the path was wet—there were foot-marks of a *very* small person.

Lucie ran on, and on.

THE path ended under a big rock. The grass was short and green, and there were clothes-props cut from bracken stems, with lines of plaited rushes, and a heap of tiny clothes pins—but no pocket-handkerchiefs!

But there was something else—a door! straight into the hill; and inside it some one was singing—

'Lily-white and clean, oh!
With little frills between, oh!
    Smooth and hot—red rusty spot
Never here be seen, oh!'

LUCIE, knocked—once—twice, and interrupted the song. A little frightened voice called out 'Who's that?'

Lucie opened the door: and what do you think there was inside the hill?—a nice clean kitchen with a flagged floor and wooden beams—just like any other farm kitchen. Only the ceiling was so low that Lucie's head nearly touched it; and the pots and pans were small, and so was everything there.

THERE was a nice hot singey smell; and at the table, with an iron in her hand stood a very stout short person staring anxiously at Lucie.

Her print gown was tucked up, and she was wearing a large apron over her striped petticoat. Her little black nose went sniffle, sniffle, snuffle, and her eyes went twinkle, twinkle; and underneath her cap—where Lucie had yellow curls—that little person had PRICKLES!

'WHO are you?' said Lucie. 'Have you seen my pocket-handkins?'

The little person made a bob-curt-sey—'Oh, yes, if you please'm; my name is Mrs. Tiggy-winkle; oh, yes if you please'm, I'm an excellent clear-starcher!' And she took something out of a clothes-basket, and spread it on the ironing-blanket.

'WHAT'S that thing?' said Lucie—
'that's not my pocket-handkin?'

'Oh no, if you please'm; that's a
little scarlet waist-coat belonging to
Cock Robin!'

And she ironed it and folded it, and
put it on one side.

THEN she took something else off
a clothes-horse—

'That isn't my pinny?' said Lucie.

'Oh no, if you please'm; that's a
damask table-cloth belonging to Jenny
Wren; look how it's stained with cur-
rant wine! It's very bad to wash!' said
Mrs. Tiggy-winkle.

MRS. TIGGY-WINKLE'S nose went sniffle, sniffle, snuffle, and her eyes went twinkle, twinkle; and she fetched another hot iron from the fire.

'THERE'S one of my pocket-handkins!' cried Lucie—'and there's
my pinny!'

Mrs. Tiggy-winkle ironed it, and
goffered it, and shook out the frills.

'Oh that *is* lovely!' said Lucie.

'AND what are those long yellow things with fingers like gloves?'

'Oh, that's a pair of stockings belonging to Sally Henny-penny—look how she's worn the heels out with scratching in the yard! She'll very soon go barefoot!' said Mrs. Tiggy-winkle.

'WHY, there's another handker-sniff—but it isn't mine; it's red?'

'Oh no, if you please'm; that one belongs to old Mrs. Rabbit; and it *did* so smell of onions! I've had to wash it separately, I can't get out the smell.'

'There's another one of mine,' said Lucie.

'WHAT are those funny little white things?'

'That's a pair of mittens belonging to Tabby Kitten; I only have to iron them; she washes them herself.'

'There's my last pocket-handkin!' said Lucie.

'AND what are you dipping into the basin of starch?'

'They're little dicky shirt-fronts belonging to Tom Titmouse—most terrible particular!' said Mrs. Tiggy-winkle. 'Now I've finished my ironing; I'm going to air some clothes.'

'WHAT are these dear soft fluffy things?' said Lucie.

'Oh those are woolly coats belonging to the little lambs at Skelghyl.'

'Will their jackets take off?' asked Lucie.

'Oh yes, if you please'm; look at the sheep-mark on the shoulder. And here's one marked for Gatesgarth, and three that come from Little-town. They're *always* marked at washing!' said Mrs. Tiggy-winkle.

AND she hung up all sorts and sizes
of clothes—small brown coats of
mice; and one velvety black mole-skin
waist-coat; and a red tail-coat with no
tail belonging to Squirrel Nutkin; and
a very much shrunk blue jacket belonging to Peter Rabbit; and a petticoat, not marked, that had gone lost in
the washing—and at last the basket
was empty!

THEN Mrs. Tiggy-winkle made
tea—a cup for herself and a cup
for Lucie. They sat before the fire on
a bench and looked sideways at one
another. Mrs. Tiggy-winkle's hand,
holding the tea-cup, was very very
brown, and very very wrinkly with the
soap-suds; and all through her gown
and her cap, there were *hair-pins* sticking wrong end out; so that Lucie
didn't like to sit too near her.

WHEN they had finished tea, they tied up the clothes in bundles; and Lucie's pocket-handkerchiefs were folded up inside her clean pinny, and fastened with a silver safety-pin.

And then they made up the fire with turf, and came out and locked the door, and hid the key under the door-sill.

THEN away down the hill trotted
Lucie and Mrs. Tiggy-winkle with
the bundles of clothes!

All the way down the path little
animals came out of the fern to meet
them; the very first that they met were
Peter Rabbit and Benjamin Bunny!

A ND she gave them their nice clean clothes; and all the little animals and birds were so very much obliged to dear Mrs. Tiggy-winkle.

SO that at the bottom of the hill
when they came to the stile, there
was nothing left to carry except Lucie's
one little bundle.

LUCIE scrambled up the stile with the bundle in her hand; and then she turned to say 'Good-night,' and to thank the washer-woman—But what a *very* odd thing! Mrs. Tiggy-winkle had not waited either for thanks or for the washing bill!

She was running running running up the hill—and where was her white frilled cap? and her shawl? and her gown—and her petticoat?

A ND *how* small she had grown—
and *how* brown—and covered with
PRICKLES!

Why! Mrs. Tiggy-winkle was nothing but a HEDGEHOG.

★   ★   ★   ★   ★

(Now some people say that little Lucie had been
asleep upon the stile—but then how could she have
found three clean pocket-handkins and a pinny, pinned
with a silver safety-pin?

And besides—*I* have seen that door into the back
of the hill called Cat Bells—and besides *I* am very
well acquainted with dear Mrs. Tiggy-winkle!)

The Tale of Jemima Puddle-Duck

WHAT a funny sight it is to see a brood of ducklings with a hen! —Listen to the story of Jemima Puddle-duck, who was annoyed because the farmer's wife would not let her hatch her own eggs.

HER sister-in-law, Mrs. Rebeccah Puddle-duck, was perfectly willing to leave the hatching to some one else—'I have not the patience to sit on a nest for twenty-eight days; and no more have you, Jemima. You would let them go cold; you know you would!'

'I wish to hatch my own eggs; I will hatch them all by myself,' quacked Jemima Puddle-duck.

S HE tried to hide her eggs; but they were always found and carried off.

Jemima Puddle-duck became quite desperate. She determined to make a nest right away from the farm.

SHE set off on a fine spring afternoon along the cart-road that leads
over the hill.

She was wearing a shawl and a poke
bonnet.

W HEN she reached the top of the
hill, she saw a wood in the
distance.

She thought that it looked a safe
quiet spot.

JEMIMA PUDDLE-DUCK was not much in the habit of flying. She ran downhill a few yards flapping her shawl, and then she jumped off into the air.

SHE flew beautifully when she had
got a good start.

She skimmed along over the tree-
tops until she saw an open place in
the middle of the wood, where the
trees and brushwood had been cleared.

JEMIMA alighted rather heavily, and
began to waddle about in search of
a convenient dry nesting-place. She

rather fancied a tree-stump amongst some tall fox-gloves.

But—seated upon the stump, she was startled to find an elegantly dressed gentleman reading a newspaper.

He had black prick ears and sandy coloured whiskers.

'Quack?' said Jemima Puddle-duck, with her head and her bonnet on one side—'Quack?'

THE gentleman raised his eyes above his newspaper and looked curiously at Jemima—

'Madam, have you lost your way?' said he. He had a long bushy tail which he was sitting upon, as the stump was somewhat damp.

Jemima thought him mighty civil and handsome. She explained that she had not lost her way, but that she was trying to find a convenient dry nesting-place.

'AH! is that so? indeed!' said the gentleman with sandy whiskers, looking curiously at Jemima. He folded up the newspaper, and put it in his coat-tail pocket.

Jemima complained of the superfluous hen.

'Indeed! how interesting! I wish I could meet with that fowl. I would teach it to mind its own business!'

'BUT as to a nest—there is no difficulty: I have a sackful of feathers in my wood-shed. No, my dear madam, you will be in nobody's way. You may sit there as long as you like,' said the bushy long-tailed gentleman.

He led the way to a very retired, dismal-looking house amongst the foxgloves.

It was built of faggots and turf, and there were two broken pails, one on top of another, by way of a chimney.

'THIS is my summer residence; you would not find my earth—my winter house—so convenient,' said the hospitable gentleman.

There was a tumble-down shed at the back of the house, made of old soap-boxes. The gentleman opened the door, and showed Jemima in.

THE shed was almost quite full of feathers—it was almost suffocating; but it was comfortable and very soft.

Jemima Puddle-duck was rather surprised to find such a vast quantity of feathers. But it was very comfortable; and she made a nest without any trouble at all.

WHEN she came out, the sandy
whiskered gentleman was sitting
on a log reading the newspaper—at
least he had it spread out, but he was
looking over the top of it.

He was so polite, that he seemed
almost sorry to let Jemima go home
for the night. He promised to take
great care of her nest until she came
back again next day.

He said he loved eggs and ducklings;
he should be proud to see a fine nestful
in his wood-shed.

JEMIMA PUDDLE-DUCK came
every afternoon; she laid nine eggs
in the nest. They were greeny white
and very large. The foxy gentleman
admired them immensely. He used to
turn them over and count them when
Jemima was not there.

At last Jemima told him that she
intended to begin to sit next day—
'and I will bring a bag of corn with
me, so that I need never leave my nest
until the eggs are hatched. They might
catch cold,' said the conscientious
Jemima.

'MADAM, I beg you not to trouble yourself with a bag; I will provide oats. But before you commence your tedious sitting, I intend to give you a treat. Let us have a dinner-party all to ourselves!

'May I ask you to bring up some herbs from the farm-garden to make a savoury omelette? Sage and thyme, and mint and two onions, and some parsley. I will provide lard for the stuff—lard for the omelette,' said the hospitable gentleman with sandy whiskers.

JEMIMA PUDDLE-DUCK was a simpleton: not even the mention of sage and onions made her suspicious.

She went round the farm-garden, nibbling off snippets of all the different sorts of herbs that are used for stuffing roast duck.

A ND she waddled into the kitchen, and got two onions out of a basket.

The collie-dog Kep met her coming out, ‘What are you doing with those onions? Where do you go every afternoon by yourself, Jemima Puddle-duck?’

Jemima was rather in awe of the collie; she told him the whole story.

The collie listened, with his wise head on one side; he grinned when she described the polite gentleman with sandy whiskers.

HE asked several questions about the wood, and about the exact position of the house and shed.

Then he went out, and trotted down the village. He went to look for two fox-hound puppies who were out at walk with the butcher.

JEMIMA PUDDLE-DUCK went up the cart-road for the last time, on a sunny afternoon. She was rather burdened with the bunches of herbs and two onions in a bag.

She flew over the wood, and alighted opposite the house of the bushy long-tailed gentleman.

HE was sitting on a log; he sniffed
the air, and kept glancing uneasily
round the wood. When Jemima
alighted he quite jumped.

'Come into the house as soon as you
have looked at your eggs. Give me the
herbs for the omelette. Be sharp!'

He was rather abrupt. Jemima
Puddle-duck had never heard him
speak like that.

She felt surprised, and uncomfort-
able.

WHILE she was inside she heard pattering feet round the back of the shed. Some one with a black nose sniffed at the bottom of the door, and then locked it.

Jemima became much alarmed.

A MOMENT afterwards there were most awful noises—barking, baying, growls and howls, squealing and groans.

And nothing more was ever seen of that foxy-whiskered gentleman.

PRESENTLY Kep opened the door of the shed, and let out Jemima Puddle-duck.

Unfortunately the puppies rushed in and gobbled up all the eggs before she could stop them.

He had a bite on his ear and both the puppies were limping.

JEMIMA PUDDLE-DUCK was es-
corted home in tears on account of
those eggs.

SHE laid some more in June, and she was permitted to keep them herself: but only four of them hatched.

Jemima Puddle-duck said that it was because of her nerves; but she had always been a bad sitter.

THE TALE OF
THE FLOPSY BUNNIES

IT is said that the effect of eating too much lettuce is 'soporific.'

I have never felt sleepy after eating lettuces; but then *I* am not a rabbit.

They certainly had a very soporific effect upon the Flopsy Bunnies!

WHEN Benjamin Bunny grew up, he married his Cousin Flopsy. They had a large family, and they were very improvident and cheerful.

I do not remember the separate names of their children; they were generally called the 'Flopsy Bunnies.'

AS there was not always quite enough to eat,—Benjamin used to borrow cabbages from Flopsy's brother, Peter Rabbit, who kept a nursery garden.

SOMETIMES Peter Rabbit had no cabbages to spare.

WHEN this happened, the Flopsy
Bunnies went across the field to a
rubbish heap, in the ditch outside Mr.
McGregor's garden.

MR. McGREGOR'S rubbish heap was a mixture. There were jam pots and paper bags, and mountains of chopped grass from the mowing machine (which always tasted oily), and some rotten vegetable marrows and an old boot or two. One day—oh joy!— there were a quantity of overgrown lettuces, which had 'shot' into flower.

THE Flopsy Bunnies simply stuffed lettuces. By degrees, one after another, they were overcome with slumber, and lay down in the mown grass.

Benjamin was not so much overcome as his children. Before going to sleep he was sufficiently wide awake to put a paper bag over his head to keep off the flies.

THE little Flopsy Bunnies slept delightfully in the warm sun. From the lawn beyond the garden came the distant clackctty sound of the mowing machine. The bluebottles buzzed about the wall, and a little old mouse picked over the rubbish among the jam pots.

(I can tell you her name, she was called Thomasina Tittlemouse, a woodmouse with a long tail.)

SHE rustled across the paper bag, and awakened Benjamin Bunny.

The mouse apologized profusely, and said that she knew Peter Rabbit.

WHILE she and Benjamin were talking, close under the wall, they heard a heavy tread above their heads; and suddenly Mr. McGregor emptied out a sackful of lawn mowings right upon the top of the sleeping Flopsy Bunnies! Benjamin shrank down under his paper bag. The mouse hid in a jam pot.

THE little rabbits smiled sweetly in their sleep under the shower of grass; they did not awake because the lettuces had been so soporific.

They dreamt that their mother Flopsy was tucking them up in a hay bed.

Mr. McGregor looked down after emptying his sack. He saw some funny little brown tips of ears sticking up through the lawn mowings. He stared at them for some time.

PRESENTLY a fly settled on one of them and it moved.

Mr. McGregor climbed down on to the rubbish heap—

'One, two, three, four! five! six leetle rabbits!' said he as he dropped them into his sack. The Flopsy Bunnies dreamt that their mother was turning them over in bed. They stirred a little in their sleep, but still they did not wake up.

MR. McGREGOR tied up the sack and left it on the wall.

He went to put away the mowing machine.

WHILE he was gone, Mrs. Flopsy
Bunny (who had remained at
home) came across the field.

She looked suspiciously at the sack
and wondered where everybody was?

THEN the mouse came out of her
jam pot, and Benjamin took the
paper bag off his head, and they told
the doleful tale.

Benjamin and Flopsy were in de-
spair, they could not undo the string.

But Mrs. Tittlemouse was a resource-
ful person. She nibbled a hole in the
bottom corner of the sack.

THE little rabbits were pulled out
and pinched to wake them.

Their parents stuffed the empty sack
with three rotten vegetable marrows,
an old blacking-brush and two decayed
turnips.

T HEN they all hid under a bush and watched for Mr. McGregor.

MR. McGREGOR came back and picked up the sack, and carried it off.

He carried it hanging down, as if it were rather heavy.

The Flopsy Bunnies followed at a safe distance.

T HEY watched him go into his
house.

And then they crept up to the
window to listen.

MR. McGREGOR threw down the sack on the stone floor in a way that would have been extremely painful to the Flopsy Bunnies, if they had happened to have been inside it.

They could hear him drag his chair on the flags, and chuckle—

'One, two, three, four, five, six leetle rabbits!' said Mr. McGregor.

'EH? What's that? What have they been spoiling now?' enquired Mrs. McGregor.

'One, two, three, four, five, six leetle fat rabbits!' repeated Mr. McGregor, counting on his fingers—'one, two, three—'

'Don't you be silly; what do you mean, you silly old man?'

'In the sack! one, two, three, four, five, six!' replied Mr. McGregor.

(The youngest Flopsy Bunny got upon the window-sill.)

MRS. McGREGOR took hold of the sack and felt it. She said she could feel six, but they must be *old* rabbits, because they were so hard and all different shapes.

'Not fit to eat; but the skins will do fine to line my old cloak.'

'Line your old cloak?' shouted Mr. McGregor—'I shall sell them and buy myself baccy!'

'Rabbit tobacco! I shall skin them and cut off their heads.'

MRS. McGREGOR untied the sack and put her hand inside.

When she felt the vegetables she became very very angry. She said that Mr. McGregor had ' done it a purpose.'

AND Mr. McGregor was very angry
too. One of the rotten marrows
came flying through the kitchen window, and hit the youngest Flopsy
Bunny.

It was rather hurt.

THEN Benjamin and Flopsy thought that it was time to go home.

SO Mr. McGregor did not get his tobacco, and Mrs. McGregor did not get her rabbit skins.

But next Christmas Thomasina Tittlemouse got a present of enough rabbit-wool to make herself a cloak and a hood, and a handsome muff and a pair of warm mittens.